The Midnight Feast

First published in Great Britain by Andersen Press Ltd. in 1996
First published in Picture Lions in 1997
1 3 5 7 9 10 8 6 4 2
ISBN: 0 00 664623-9
Picture Lions is an imprint of the Children's Division,
part of HarperCollins Publishers Ltd.
Text copyright © Lindsay Camp 1996
Illustrations copyright © Tony Ross 1996
The author and illustrator assert the moral right to be identified as the author and illustrator of the work.
A CIP catalogue record for this title is available from the British Library.
All rights reserved. No part of this publication may be reproduced, stored in a retrieval system
or transmitted in any form or by any means, electronic, mechanical, photocopying,
recording or otherwise, without the prior permission of HarperCollins Publishers Ltd,
77-85 Fulham Palace Road, Hammersmith, London W6 8JB.
Printed and bound in Singapore by Imago.

The Midnight Feast

Written by Lindsay Camp
Illustrated by Tony Ross

PictureLions
An Imprint of HarperCollins*Publishers*

At bathtime, Alice whispered something to Freddie.

What was that?

Nothing.

What is a midnight feast?

Shhhh!

"Night night, love," said Mum, stretching to kiss Alice in the top bunk.

"Night night, poppet," she said, bending to kiss Freddie in the bottom bunk.

As soon as Mum was gone,

Alice climbed out of bed.

Come on, we've got to get ready.

She pulled the quilt off Freddie's bed and spread it on the floor.

Alice took a plastic bag from under the bunks and
looked inside.

We need some more
food. I don't think
beautiful princesses
like salt and vinegar
crisps.

What *do* they like?

Freddie crept downstairs...

...and went to look for pomegranates and lobsters.

Mum was tidying the playroom...

...and he didn't think she heard him.

When Freddie got back, Alice was sitting on his quilt.

She took the lobsters and pomegranates from him.

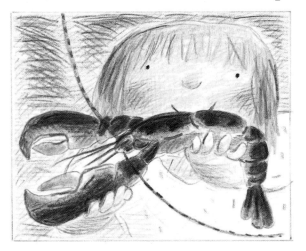

Alice wriggled a bit on Freddie's quilt.

Freddie crept downstairs...

...and went to hunt for a soft golden cushion.

A floorboard creaked, but Mum was in the kitchen now...

...and she was humming to herself quite loudly.

When he got back, Alice was just making sure that one of the pomegranates was sweet enough.

Alice licked juice off her chin, and Freddie gave her the soft golden cushion.

Freddie hurried downstairs, and nearly tripped
over Beelzebub.

But Mum had turned on the TV...   ...so she didn't hear.

When Freddie got back, Alice was sitting on the soft
golden cushion, licking one of the lobsters.
The last one.

Alice took the enchanted musical box from him.

Freddie sat down next to Alice...   ...and waited.

A few minutes passed.

It's all right. I don't think she'll be very hungry. And if she is, I suppose she could eat the salt and vinegar crisps.

Freddie waited some more.
"When will she come?" he yawned. "It must be midnight now."

But Alice didn't answer.

A little later, the door opened, and someone came in.
She covered Alice with a quilt, and kissed her. She lifted
Freddie gently into bed and covered him too. Then she
kissed him. Freddie opened his eyes for a moment.
"I knew you'd come," he whispered, "my sister said so."

And then Freddie closed his eyes and went back to sleep.

And dreamed all night of a beautiful princess
holding him in her arms.

Collins
Picture Lions

Have you read all these stories by Tony Ross?